Hiding Hopcyn

Story: Eiry Palfrey

Illustrated by Graham Howells

A translation by Viv Sayer

Published in 2006 by Pont Books, an imprint of Gomer Press,
Llandysul, Ceredigion, SA44 4JL

ISBN 1 84323 712 1
ISBN 13-978 1843237129

This book was first published in Welsh by Gomer Press in 2005 under the title 'Melangell'.

A CIP record for this title is available from the British Library.

This book is published with the financial support of the Welsh Books Council.

Printed and bound in Wales at
Gomer Press, Llandysul, Ceredigion

'Guess what!' said Rhian Rabbit. 'I've got a new friend! A girl, the same age as me.'

'A human being?' Hopcyn Hare stared in surprise. 'You'd better be careful, Rhian. People can be really cruel!'

'But Melangell is kind and gentle,' said Rhian. 'Why don't you come and meet her!'

'Please, can we come too?' squeaked Morys Mouse
and Heulwen Hedgehog.

'Of course,' said Rhian.
'Melangell likes animals.'
And off they scurried to Pennant Forest. At first Hopcyn hung
behind – he was jealous of Rhian's new friend – but he was
curious too and ran after the others on the tips of his paws.

In a clearing in the forest sat a pretty young girl.

'She's talking to someone,' whispered Heulwen.

'God, I expect,' said Rhian.

'I can't see anybody,' squeaked Morys.

'Nobody can see God,' explained Rhian. 'But Melangell knows that he's there.'

Suddenly Melangell caught sight of them. 'Rhian!' she said. 'Are you going to introduce me to your friends?'

'This is Morys,' said Rhian shyly, 'and this is Heulwen.'

Melangell smiled. 'I can see someone else, can't I? Hiding behind that tree?'

Rhian turned to see Hopcyn peeping out from behind a tree trunk.

'Oh, that's Hopcyn Hare,' she said. 'He's really shy.'

Hopcyn scampered off at once, most put out that he'd been spotted.

6

At a large castle nearby Prince Brochwel was getting ready for the chase. He sounded his hunting horn and away went the riders and their hounds, galloping full pelt towards the forest.

Hopcyn was playing a game of tag with Rhian. They were taking turns at running into the woods to hide. Suddenly he heard the sound of angry barking and saw two fierce hunting dogs racing towards him.

Hopcyn was terrified. He ran for his life, going deeper and deeper into the forest. The dogs were snapping at his heels and getting closer and closer with every bound. He could feel their hot breath on the back of his neck.

Just as he thought he couldn't run any further, Hopcyn reached the spot where Melangell was sitting. He leapt into her lap, trembling all over.

'Hopcyn,' she said. 'Whatever is the matter?'

The hounds raced into the clearing, barking furiously. Melangell fixed them with a look. At once the dogs froze to the spot.

Melangell soothed Hopcyn, stroking him gently and hiding him in the folds of her long sleeve.

Just then Brochwel galloped into the clearing. 'Have you seen a hare running through these woods?' he demanded.

Melangell did not reply.

Hopcyn poked the tip of his nose out from under Melangell's sleeve. 'There he is,' shouted Brochwel. 'After him!'

But the hounds could not move. They were like two statues.

'This is my friend Hopcyn,' said Melangell. 'You mustn't hurt him.'

Brochwel got down from his horse. 'This forest belongs to me,' he said. 'You have no right to be here. Who are you, anyway?'

'My name is Melangell. I'm not doing any harm, just saying my prayers and talking to my friends. Why do you have to hunt them? They haven't done anything to you. You should be ashamed of yourself.'

Brochwel was sorry that he'd upset Melangell. 'You are right,' he said, 'I won't ever hunt in Pennant Forest again, and you have my permission to stay here for as long as you like.'

Melangell smiled, and once again the hounds were able to move. They ran away, their tails between their legs.

Nowadays a church stands in Pennant Melangell and, to this very day, the local people have a special name for the hare. They call him 'Melangell's baby lamb'.